Little Vampire
and the
Midnight Bear

Mary DeBall Kwitz
pictures by S. D. Schindler

PUFFIN BOOKS

For my mother, my friend,
Mary O'Connor DeBall, 1893–1993
M.D.K.

PUFFIN BOOKS
Published by the Penguin Group
Penguin Putnam Inc., 375 Hudson Street, New York, New York 10014, U.S.A.
Penguin Books Ltd, 27 Wrights Lane, London W8 5TZ, England
Penguin Books Australia Ltd, Ringwood, Victoria, Australia
Penguin Books Canada Ltd, 10 Alcorn Avenue, Toronto, Ontario, Canada M4V 3B2
Penguin Books (N.Z.) Ltd, 182-190 Wairau Road, Auckland 10, New Zealand

Penguin Books Ltd, Registered Offices: Harmondsworth, Middlesex, England

First published in the United States of America by Dial Books for Young Readers,
a division of Penguin Books USA, Inc., 1995
Published in a Puffin Easy-to-Read edition by Puffin Books,
a member of Penguin Putnam Books for Young Readers, 1998

1 3 5 7 9 10 8 6 4 2

Text copyright © Mary DeBall Kwitz, 1995
Illustrations copyright © S. D. Schindler, 1995
All rights reserved

THE LIBRARY OF CONGRESS HAS CATALOGED THE DIAL EDITION AS FOLLOWS:
Kwitz, Mary DeBall.
Little Vampire and the Midnight Bear / by Mary DeBall Kwitz;
pictures by S. D. Schindler.—1st ed.   p.   cm.
Summary: Little Vampire discovers that he can fly when he needs to save his baby
sister from the dreadful Midnight Bear.
ISBN 0-8037-1528-5 (trade).—ISBN 0-8037-1529-3 (library)
[1. Vampires—Fiction. 2. Bears—Fiction. 3. Flight—Fiction. 4. Family life—Fiction.]
I. Schindler, S. D., ill. II. Title.
PZ7.K976Lm 1995 [E]—dc20 94-29327 CIP AC

Puffin Easy-to-Read ISBN 0-14-130233-X
Puffin® and Easy-to-Read® are registered trademarks of Penguin Books USA Inc.

Printed in Hong Kong

Reading Level 2.3

COUSIN BUBBA

"Come on, Little Vampire,"
yelled Cousin Bubba.
"Let's find the cave of the
Midnight Bear."

"Who is the Midnight Bear?"

asked Little Vampire.

"He is the biggest, meanest bear

in the whole world," said Cousin Bubba.

"What does he do?"

asked Little Vampire.

"He eats dumb little kids,"
said Cousin Bubba.
"But don't worry.
If the Midnight Bear chases us,
we can fly away."

"I don't know how to fly,"

said Little Vampire.

"And I can't leave.

My birthday party is tonight."

"Ha! Ha!" laughed Cousin Bubba.

"Wait until you see *my* present!"

Cousin Bubba climbed up on a rock

and jumped into the air.

"See you at the party, Little Stupid,"

he yelled.

Then he did a figure eight

over the house.

THE BIRTHDAY WISH

"Make a wish and blow out the candles,
Little Vampire," said Mama.

Little Vampire closed his eyes
and said softly, "I wish—
I wish I had a puppy."
Then he blew real hard.

"You blew them all out," said Grandpa.
"Your wish will come true."

Grandpa's gift was a sleeping bag.

"When you learn to fly," he said,

"you can visit me and sleep over."

Little Vampire opened

Cousin Bubba's gift next.

A hairy spider jumped out of the box.

"Ha! Ha!" laughed Cousin Bubba.

Mama and Papa gave him a vampire cape.

It was just like Papa's cape.

"You can wear it

when you learn to fly," said Mama.

"Try it on," said Papa.

Little Vampire put on his new cape.

Then he looked all around the room.

There were no more presents.

"Gramps," he said,

"I blew out all the candles,

but I did not get my wish."

"Ha! Ha!" laughed Cousin Bubba.

WHO'S A BABY?

"Papa and I are flying
to the Vampire Society meeting,"
said Mama.
"Can I come too? *Please!*"
begged Little Vampire.

"You haven't learned to fly yet,"
said Mama. "You must stay home
with Baby Vampira.
Grandpa lives right next door.
He has promised to fly over
and check on you."

"I am not a baby,"
cried Little Vampire.
"I can fly with you. Watch me, Mama."
He climbed up on the kitchen stool
and jumped into the air.

Bang! He knocked the stool over.

Kerplunk! He hit the floor.

"Be careful, dear," said Mama.

She gave Baby Vampira

a bottle of warm grasshopper juice.

Then she burped her and

changed her diaper.

"Pee-hew!" said Little Vampire.

"Stinky baby sister.

I wish you were a puppy."

"Good-bye, Little Vampire," said Mama.
"Mind your grandpa
and don't tease the baby,"
she said as she flew out the window.

"Lock the shutters," said Papa.
"And do not open them
for anyone but Grandpa," he said.
Then he flew out the window.

KNOCK, KNOCK, WHO'S THERE?

Little Vampire closed the shutters
and locked them tight.
Then he ate a large bowl
of Caterpillar Crunch Cereal.
After eating he brushed his fangs
until they sparkled.

CLUNK! CLUNK! CLUNK!

Someone was banging on the shutters.

"Nobody's home," Little Vampire yelled.

"Open up, Sonny."

"Gramps!" cried Little Vampire.

He opened the shutters and Grandpa made

a one-point landing on the table.

He hugged Little Vampire.

"How is my favorite grandson?"

He kissed the baby.

"Hello, my little tootsie-wootsie."

Little Vampire giggled.

Grandpa liked to talk silly.

They got out the doodlebug board

and played until each had won

three games.

Then they snuggled

in front of the fire

and ate Beetle Brittle Bars.

"Gramps," said Little Vampire,

"did you ever see the Midnight Bear?"

"Sure did, Sonny," said Grandpa.
"One night when I was about your age
the Midnight Bear almost caught me."

"What happened?" cried Little Vampire.

"I made my fierce, horrible
vampire face," said Grandpa.
"And I growled and howled.

I chased that Midnight Bear
back where he belonged."

Grandpa shook out his cape.

"Time to fly home," he said.

"Mama and Papa will be back soon.

Don't forget to lock the shutters,"

he said as he flew out the window.

THE MIDNIGHT BEAR

Little Vampire practiced making
scary faces in the mirror.

The baby was laughing and
gurgling in her playpen.

"If you were a puppy, we could play,"
said Little Vampire.
"But you're all wrinkled
and you're burping bubbles.
You're *icky*!"

He made a mean vampire face
and growled at her.

Baby Vampira turned red and bawled.

"Don't cry," Little Vampire begged.

The baby shut her eyes and screamed.

Suddenly Little Vampire heard
snuffling and sniffing at the window.

"I HEAR THE CRY
OF A BABY VAMPIRE,"
rumbled a voice, loud as thunder.
"I SMELL SOMETHING
GOOD TO EAT!"

"Oh, no!" cried Little Vampire.

He had forgotten to lock the shutters.

He ran to the window.

There stood the Midnight Bear!

He was drooling!

The Midnight Bear leaped into the room.

He looked at the playpen.

"WHAT A TENDER MOUTHFUL!"
he roared.

34

Little Vampire forgot

that he could not fly.

He flew to the playpen

and snatched up his baby sister.

Then he flew out the window
and zoomed up to the rooftop.

The Midnight Bear started climbing
up the drainpipe after them.

Little Vampire made a fierce,
horrible vampire face and growled:
"GRRRRRRRRRRRRRrrrrrrrrrrrrrr!"
He gnashed his fangs and howled:
"OOOOOOOOOOOOOOoooooooooooooooo!"

The Midnight Bear let go of
the drainpipe and covered his ears.
He fell to the ground.

"Go away!" yelled Little Vampire.
The Midnight Bear picked himself up
and ran back to his cave in the woods.

GRANDPA'S SURPRISE

The next night

Little Vampire called Grandpa.

"Guess what?" he said. "I can fly!"

"Great, Sonny!" said Grandpa.

"Fly over to my house

and I will make your favorite dinner."

Little Vampire put on his vampire cape

and picked up his sleeping bag.

"Good-bye, Mama and Papa," he said.

Cousin Bubba was waiting outside.

"Hey, Little Stupid!" he yelled.

"Let's catch flies

and feed them to your spider."

"I am busy," said Little Vampire.

"Watch this, Cousin Bubba."

He flapped his vampire cape

and zoomed up to Grandpa's roof.

"HA! HA! Cousin Bubba," he shouted.

Then he did a figure eight

around the chimney.

Grandpa was waiting for him.

They had rat-tail soup and

bat-wing sandwiches on rye bread

for dinner.

Little Vampire was just biting into

his sandwich when he heard a noise.

46

It was a snuffling and a sniffing sound
in the bedroom.

"Gramps," he said softly,

"do you hear a scary noise?"

"Sure do, Sonny," said Grandpa.

They tiptoed to the bedroom
and peeked in.
"Oh!" cried Little Vampire.
He sat down on the floor
and the Scary Noise
jumped into his lap
and licked his nose.